P9-CFL-777

The Boxcar Children Mysteries

The Boxcar Children
Surprise Island
The Yellow House Mystery
Mystery Ranch
Mike's Mystery
Blue Bay Mystery
The Woodshed Mystery
The Lighthouse Mystery
Mountain Top Mystery
Schoolhouse Mystery
Caboose Mystery
Houseboat Mystery
Snowbound Mystery
Tree House Mystery
Bicycle Mystery
Mystery in the Sand
Mystery Behind the Wall
Bus Station Mystery
Benny Uncovers a Mystery
The Haunted Cabin Mystery
The Deserted Library Mystery
The Animal Shelter Mystery
The Old Motel Mystery
The Mystery of the Hidden Painting
The Amusement Park Mystery
The Mystery of the Mixed-Up Zoo
The Camp-out Mystery
The Mystery Girl
The Mystery Cruise
The Disappearing Friend Mystery
The Mystery of the Singing Ghost
Mystery in the Snow
The Pizza Mystery
The Mystery Horse
The Mystery at the Dog Show
The Castle Mystery
The Mystery of the Lost Village
The Mystery on the Ice (Winter Special)
The Mystery of the Purple Pool
The Ghost Ship Mystery
The Mystery in Washington, DC (Spring Special)
The Canoe Trip Mystery
The Mystery of the Hidden Beach
The Mystery of the Missing Cat

THE MYSTERY OF THE MISSING CAT

created by
GERTRUDE CHANDLER WARNER

Illustrated by Charles Tang

SCHOLASTIC INC.
New York Toronto London Auckland Sydney

No part of this publication may be reproduced in whole or in part, or stored in a retrieval system, or transmitted in any form or by any means, electronic, mechanical, photocopying, recording, or otherwise, without written permission of the publisher. For information regarding permission, write to Albert Whitman & Company, 6340 Oakton Street, Morton Grove, IL 60053-2723.

ISBN 0-590-47536-3

Copyright © 1994 by Albert Whitman & Company. All rights reserved.
Published by Scholastic Inc. 555 Broadway, New York, NY 10012, by arrangement with Albert Whitman & Company. THE BOXCAR CHILDREN® is a registered trademark of Albert Whitman & Company.

12 11 10 9 8 7 6 5 4 3 4 5 6 7 8 9/9

Printed in the U.S.A. 40

First Scholastic printing, September 1994

Contents

CHAPTER 1

The Missing Cat

"What are you two doing, Benny?" asked ten-year-old Violet Alden. She stood on the front steps of the old white house, watching her five-year-old brother Benny and her seven-year-old cousin, Soo Lee Alden.

Benny laughed. "We're practicing walking backward," he explained.

Soo Lee nodded and added, "When we get good enough, we're going to have a walking-backward race!"

"Benny, look out!" cried Violet. But it was too late. Benny had walked backward right into a pile of leaves.

"Oh!" said Benny, falling down. Leaves flew up and scattered everywhere. Watch, the Aldens' dog, who had been lying on the grass, gave an excited bark and raced over to the pile of leaves. He jumped in, too.

"Look, Benny," said Soo Lee. "Watch thinks you're playing a game!" She picked up a handful of leaves and threw them in the air. Watch leaped up and tried to catch them, barking the whole time.

Violet smiled as she watched Benny and Soo Lee. Then Benny stopped. He looked down at the scattered leaves. "Uh-oh!" he said. "These are the leaves that Henry and Jessie raked up this morning." Henry, who was fourteen, and Jessie, who was twelve, were the oldest of the four Alden children.

"Don't worry," called Henry. A moment later he and Jessie came outside to join the others. "We can rake those up again in no time."

"Yes, if we all do it together," said Violet.

Benny jumped out of the leaves. "I'll get the rakes," he said.

Benny hurried away and soon returned with the rakes. The five children set to work and soon had all the leaves in a big pile again.

"Whew," said Benny. "Jumping in the leaves was fun. But raking them up is hard work!"

"Are you hungry, Benny?" Jessie teased her brother. The others all laughed when Benny nodded. Benny was always hungry.

Benny laughed, too. "Yes," he answered. "I'm very hungry."

"I think it's time for a snack," said Henry. "Come on!" He led the way through the house to the big kitchen in the back. Mrs. McGregor, the housekeeper, was sitting at the kitchen table drinking tea with a curly-haired woman wearing a dark blue dress with a white collar.

"Hello, children," said Mrs. McGregor, her cheerful face breaking into a broad smile. "This is a friend of mine, Mrs. Valentine.

She's just come over to tell me the good news. Her niece, Whitney, is coming to visit!"

"She's a first-year student at college," said Mrs. Valentine. "I hope you'll all be able to meet her."

Mrs. McGregor introduced the Aldens.

"And Watch," added Benny quickly, pointing to the small terrier who was sitting at his feet.

"And, of course, Watch," agreed Mrs. McGregor.

Mrs. Valentine said hello to everyone and leaned over to pat the dog's head. "How do you do, Watch?" she asked. Watch wagged his tail happily.

"He's a wonderful dog," said Mrs. Valentine. "Does he belong to you, Benny?"

"No, we belong to him," said Benny.

Violet nodded shyly. "It's true. He found us."

As the Aldens got out cookies and milk, Soo Lee told how she had lived in Korea before Joe and Alice Alden, who were cousins of James Alden, had adopted her. Then

Henry, Jessie, Violet, and Benny told the story of how the little dog had come limping into their lives when they first became orphans and were living in an old abandoned boxcar in the woods. Jessie had pulled the thorn from the little dog's paw, and Benny had named him Watch, and he had been a good friend and watchdog ever since.

Now the old boxcar was in the yard behind the big white house where the Aldens lived with their grandfather, James Alden. They hadn't known it when they were living in the boxcar, but he had been searching and searching for them. When he'd found them at last, he had brought them all to Greenfield to live with him. He'd even brought the boxcar, too, so they could visit it whenever they wanted.

"What an amazing story," said Mrs. Valentine. "You know, it's funny, but I know a cat who found someone, too, sort of the way Watch found you."

"Really?" said Violet, forgetting her shyness. "What happened?"

"I'm the housekeeper for Mr. Woods. He lives in the big stone house at the end of Tucker Lane. He lives all alone. He never visits friends. Friends never visit him. He never goes anywhere except for walks. He just doesn't seem to like anyone."

"Doesn't he have a family?" asked Soo Lee.

"No, no one," said Mrs. Valentine. "But one day just a few months ago, he came home from one of his long walks carrying a tiny little calico kitten — white with orange and black spots. She was skinny and starving, with funny, crinkled, dirty spotted fur. Why, she was so young her eyes were still blue — kittens' eyes usually change to green or yellow when they're five or six weeks old."

"I didn't know that," said Benny.

"Poor kitten," said softhearted Violet.

"But she was a lucky kitten after all," Mrs. Valentine went on. "Because Mr. Woods kept her and fed her and nursed her back to health. He named her Spotzie, and now wherever he goes, she goes."

"That's a very nice story," said Mrs. McGregor.

Mrs. Valentine shook her head sadly. "It *was* a nice story. But a few days ago, Mr. Woods and Spotzie were sitting on the porch the way they always do in the afternoon. Mr. Woods went inside for a minute. And when he came back outside, Spotzie was gone!"

"Did she run away?" asked Jessie.

"I don't think so. Mr. Woods was only gone a minute. And he came back out and called and called for Spotzie. She always comes when she's called. But she didn't this time."

"Did Mr. Woods call the Greenfield Animal Shelter?" asked Jessie.

"He did. And he goes out every day, looking for her and calling for her. But she's just disappeared!" Mrs. Valentine frowned.

"Maybe we could help," said Henry. "Maybe we could find Spotzie for Mr. Woods."

Mrs. Valentine took a last sip of tea and stood up. "It would be a wonderful thing if you could," she told the five children. "It's upset Mr. Woods terribly. I feel sorry for that man."

"Could we come over tomorrow?" asked Jessie.

Mrs. Valentine thought for a moment, then nodded."Yes. Mr. Woods or I could show you where Spotzie was when she disappeared. My niece is coming tomorrow, so if she's arrived, you can meet her, too."

"We'd like that," said Henry. Everyone agreed that they would.

Mrs. Valentine thanked Mrs. McGregor for the tea, and left, telling the children she'd look forward to seeing them the following day.

Benny said, "Maybe Watch can use his nose and find Spotzie."

"Maybe," said Jessie.

"Oh, Benny," said Violet. "You have a milk mustache!"

Benny put his cup of milk down. Sure enough, he had milk across his upper lip.

Benny looked down at Watch, who had been drinking milk from his bowl on the floor beside the door.

"Look," he said, pointing. "Watch has a milk mustache, too!"

CHAPTER 2

The Search Begins

The next day after breakfast, the Boxcar children went to get Soo Lee. She lived with cousins Joe and Alice in an old gray shingled house on the edge of Greenfield. When Joe and Alice had decided to move to Greenfield and had bought the old house, it hadn't been as nice as it was now. The Boxcar children had even thought it was haunted — by a singing ghost!

But the children had helped fix up the old house and had solved the ghost mystery.

Now the house looked welcoming as the four children rode up on their bicycles.

Soo Lee was sitting on the steps when they arrived.

"You're right on time," she said, her eyes sparkling. She got on her bike, and soon the five of them were on their way to Mr. Woods's house to find out more about the missing cat and maybe to meet Mrs. Valentine's niece.

The day was bright and sunny. The Aldens rode their bicycles briskly through Greenfield, enjoying the feel of the air on their faces. They waved at the people they passed, who all seemed to be enjoying the day, too.

But when they reached Tucker Lane, Violet stopped her bike, a worried expression on her face.

Henry looked back. "What is it, Violet?" he asked, getting off his bicycle. The others got off their bicycles, too.

Violet bit her lip and looked down the street toward the big stone house. "Mrs. Valentine said Mr. Woods didn't like *anybody*. What if he's mean?"

The other children looked thoughtful. Then Soo Lee said, "She didn't say he was mean, did she?"

Jessie said, "No, she didn't. Maybe he's just nervous when he meets new people, Violet. Maybe he's shy."

Violet was shy herself, so she could understand how that felt. She nodded slowly and looked a little less worried. "Maybe he *is* shy," she said.

"We won't know until we get there," Henry pointed out.

"Okay," said Violet. "Let's go!" She got on her bicycle and began to pedal determinedly toward the big stone house. The others quickly followed.

As they got closer, they could see that the house didn't look so scary. The wide front porch had big wicker chairs on it. Brightly colored pillows made the chairs look even more comfortable. A table with a pot of flowers on it stood at one end of the porch, and there were hanging baskets with ferns in them all around.

"Mr. Woods may not like people, but he likes plants," Jessie observed.

They walked up the stairs and Henry knocked on the door, using the heavy old brass knocker.

No one answered. Henry knocked a second time. But still no one answered.

"Maybe no one's home," said Benny.

"Mrs. Valentine's niece *is* arriving today. Maybe she went to meet her," said Henry.

"But Mrs. Valentine said Mr. Woods never goes anywhere or talks to anybody," said Violet softly. "He must be here."

"He goes on walks," Benny reminded them. "That's how he found Spotzie."

"True," said Henry. "Maybe that's what he's doing now."

"Even if he is here, I don't think he's going to answer the door," said Soo Lee.

"Yes, we've knocked long enough," agreed Henry. "I guess we'd better go."

Suddenly, Violet said, "Did you see that?"

Everyone looked at Violet, then in the direction she was staring.

"What, Violet?" Jessie asked.

"I thought I saw someone behind the curtain at the front window," Violet said.

They all watched the window. But they couldn't see anything.

"Maybe it was a draft inside," said Henry.

"Or maybe Mr. Woods is home, like Soo Lee said, and he just won't answer the door," said Jessie.

"Do you think he has been watching us the whole time?" asked Benny.

"I don't know, Benny," said Jessie.

"That's sad, if he's too shy to answer the door," said Violet. "He must miss Spotzie a lot."

"We can find Spotzie," declared Henry.

"Yes," said Violet. "Let's get started right now."

"Mrs. Valentine said Mr. Woods goes out and looks for Spotzie every day. But if he doesn't like people, I bet he hasn't asked the neighbors," said Jessie. "We can ask."

"Yes, let's do that," said Violet.

Jessie looked down the street. "There are eleven other houses on this street," said Jessie. "Soo Lee and Benny and I will go to those six houses over there. Violet, you and Henry can go to the other five houses. Then we can meet at the corner."

"Good idea, Jessie," said Henry. "Come on, Violet, let's go."

Jessie, Soo Lee, and Benny headed to the first house on their side of the street. A man in a straw hat was standing in the small rose garden in front. They asked if he'd seen a little calico cat.

"I don't like cats," he replied. "They're always digging in my garden."

"She's a *nice* cat," said Soo Lee. "I don't think she would do that."

The man looked down at Soo Lee, and the frown left his face. "Well . . . spotted, you say? I'll keep an eye out for her. But I haven't seen her."

No one was home at the next house. At

the third house, a big dog came running down to the gate, barking loudly.

"Uh-oh," said Benny, backing up. "It's a good thing Watch isn't with us!"

As if he knew who Watch was, the dog barked even more loudly.

"I don't think any cats would go *there*!" exclaimed Jessie. "Come on."

No one at the last three houses that Jessie, Benny, and Soo Lee visited had seen a little lost cat, either.

Henry and Violet didn't have any better luck. At the first house, a man holding a crying baby opened the door.

"Cats?" he said. "Who has time for cats? Besides, I'm allergic to them. So is my son." He nodded at the baby he was holding. The baby cried and cried.

"Thank you," said Violet politely.

At the next house, a young woman wearing glasses and holding a book in one hand came to the door. She pushed her glasses up the bridge of her nose with one finger and peered out at them. "Yes?"

A moment later, a big fat orange cat stuck its head out the door, too.

"Lost cat?" she said when Henry told her why they were there. "Oh, no. No cat would *dare* come around this house." She bent to pat the orange cat's head. "Malcolm here is a very tough watch cat. He wouldn't allow another cat on his property. But I'll keep my eyes open."

No one at the next three houses had seen Spotzie either, but everyone the children spoke to promised to stay on the lookout for the little calico cat.

The five children met on the corner at the end of the street.

"No luck," Jessie told Henry as he and Violet walked up.

"We didn't have any luck, either," Henry answered. "We'd better be getting home. It's almost lunch, and we've got chores to do."

The five children got on their bikes and pedaled slowly back to the big old house.

"Where could that cat have gone?" wondered Jessie.

Henry shook his head. "It's a mystery, that's for sure."

Violet, who was riding next to Soo Lee, said softly, "Poor Spotzie. She's lost and all alone."

"We'll find her soon," Soo Lee said.

"I hope so," Violet answered. "I hope so."

CHAPTER 3

A Trip to the Animal Shelter

"If I were a cat," said Jessie, passing the mashed potatoes to Benny, "and I got lost, I wonder what I would do."

Jessie, Violet, Benny, and Henry were having dinner that night with their grandfather, sitting around the table in the dining room. They'd been telling him about the mystery of the missing cat.

"I'm surprised at how quickly Spotzie disappeared from the porch," said Grandfather Alden.

"Maybe she started chasing something," said Benny. "When Watch chases squirrels, he doesn't even listen when you say his name."

From his place by the door, Watch heard his name. He pricked up his ears and tipped his head to one side as if he were thinking about what Benny had said.

"That's true, Benny," said Grandfather. "More green peas?"

"Yes, thank you," said Benny.

"What we need is a picture of Spotzie," said Jessie.

"That's a good idea, Jessie," Henry said. "Do you suppose Mr. Woods has a photograph of her?"

"If he did and we could get it, we could show it to people," said Jessie.

"Yes," said Violet. "And we could even make signs to put up. We could put them up at the animal shelter."

"And at Dr. Scott's office," said Benny. Dr. Scott was a Greenfield veterinarian who was Watch's doctor. She also helped take care of the animals at the Greenfield Animal Shelter and she had helped the Aldens with two mysteries they'd solved, one involving the animal shelter and the other a dog show that had come to Greenfield.

"That's a good idea, too, Benny. She might be able to give us some suggestions. And we need to talk to Mr. Woods," said Henry.

"We can make some signs in the morning," said Benny. "We have posterboard and markers out in the boxcar."

"We'll do that first," agreed Jessie. "Then we can put them up at the shelter and at Dr. Scott's and talk to her."

"And to Mr. Woods," Henry reminded her.

Grandfather Alden smiled at their enthusiasm. "Sounds like you have a busy day planned for tomorrow."

"Yes," said Benny. He smiled back at his grandfather. "What's for dessert?"

* * *

The four Aldens went out to their boxcar right after breakfast the next morning and began working on the signs about the missing cat.

"I don't know what Spotzie looks like, so I'm just drawing a cat with spots on her," said Violet. "Someone should be able to recognize her from that."

"That's good, Violet." Jessie looked at her sister's picture. "The important thing is to let people know to look for a lost cat."

"And who to call about her," added Henry, writing their phone number on his poster.

The Aldens were good at making signs and posters. They soon had enough for the animal shelter and the veterinarian's office and for the neighborhood where Spotzie was lost.

They put the signs in their backpacks and got ready to go look for Spotzie.

"You stay here, Watch," said Violet. "I

don't think you want to go to Dr. Scott's office."

"Watch can keep me company in the kitchen," said Mrs. McGregor. "I may even have a dog biscuit for him."

Hearing the word "biscuit," Watch trotted happily after Mrs. McGregor to the kitchen, wagging his tail.

The Aldens set off on their bicycles to put the signs up around Greenfield, heading first for the Greenfield Animal Shelter.

"Has anyone brought in a calico cat?" asked Henry when they got to the animal shelter.

The shelter attendant behind the desk looked surprised. "A calico cat? That's funny," she said. "There was a man just here, describing a cat that he'd lost that sounded a lot like yours." The attendant leaned over the counter and looked around, as if she expected the man to still be there. But the Aldens were the only ones in the waiting room.

"I wonder if that was Mr. Woods," Jessie said.

"He didn't tell me his name," the attendant said.

"Did you have his cat?" asked Violet carefully.

The attendant shook her head. "No, and I'm sorry, we don't have yours, either. No one has brought in a calico cat."

"Oh. Then, may we put this up on your bulletin board?" asked Jessie, showing the woman one of the signs they'd made.

The woman nodded approvingly. "Of course you can."

"Thank you," said Jessie. She took the sign over to the bulletin board and put it up right in the middle.

"That's a good sign. Very simple and clear," said the shelter attendant. "If we get any cats fitting that description, we'll call you."

"Thank you," said Jessie again, and the

LOST CAT

other Aldens echoed her words.

"It's funny that there are two lost cats who look alike," said Benny, as the Aldens went outside.

"Unless it's the same one," Jessie said, lost in thought.

The day was getting hot, and they began to push their bicycles slowly up the hill outside the shelter.

"Hey, Jessie, slow down!" Henry called out.

But Jessie didn't seem to hear. She just kept walking faster and faster.

"Jessie?" said Henry.

Abruptly, Jessie stopped. "Let's turn here," she said.

"But that's not the way to Dr. Scott's office," said Violet.

"Let's go a new way," said Jessie mysteriously.

Puzzled, her brother and sister agreed and turned down the street Jessie had suggested.

"Can't we go more slowly?" panted Benny.

Jessie looked back over her shoulder and stopped again.

"We're being followed," she said.

"What?" said Henry.

"Don't look," Jessie said quickly. "But there's a man back there. He started following us as soon as we came out of the animal shelter!"

CHAPTER 4

The Mysterious Stranger

"What should we do?" asked Violet.

"Let's keep walking," said Henry. "But not so fast."

The four children began to walk down the street, trying to act as if nothing was wrong.

Jessie glanced quickly over her shoulder. "He's still there."

"Why is he following us?" Benny asked.

"I don't know, Benny," Jessie answered.

"Why don't we ask him?" suggested Benny.

Jessie looked down at Benny. Suddenly she smiled. "You know, Benny, that's not a bad idea. I think we *should* ask him."

"Oh, Jessie!" gasped Violet. "Really?"

"What could happen? It's the middle of the day and we're on a street in the middle of town," Jessie pointed out sensibly.

"You're right," said Henry.

The four stopped again and looked at one another.

"Okay," said Jessie, "let's go."

The Aldens turned around and began walking back toward the man who was following them.

For a moment, he stood in the middle of the sidewalk as if he didn't know what to do. Then abruptly, he turned and began to run.

"Come on!" shouted Jessie. She jumped on her bicycle and began to pedal after the stranger. The other children did the same.

But it was no use. The man turned up a

narrow alley, leaped over a low fence, and disappeared.

The Aldens stopped by the fence, breathing hard. After they'd gotten their breath, they turned around and went back the way they'd come, heading for Dr. Scott's office.

"Did anybody recognize him?" asked Henry.

Nobody had. It had been hard to tell anything about the mysterious stranger. He'd been too far away, and even though the day had gotten hot, he was wearing a hat, a coat, dark glasses, a scarf, and baggy pants. They couldn't even tell whether he was fat or thin!

"Maybe he has something to do with Spotzie," said Jessie thoughtfully.

"But what?" asked Violet.

"I don't know," said Jessie. "I've just got a funny feeling."

The Boxcar children walked in silence for a while, thinking about what Jessie had said.

The Aldens kept a careful watch for the mysterious stranger all the way to Dr. Scott's office, but he never reappeared. When they got to the veterinarian's office, her assistant said, "Dr. Scott is very busy right now."

At that moment, Dr. Scott walked out to the waiting room with a girl holding a small dog with a bandage on its paw.

"And make sure she stays off that paw," Dr. Scott said.

"Thank you, Dr. Scott," said the girl. She and the dog went out.

Dr. Scott saw the Aldens and greeted them. "So you have a cat now, too?" she asked, seeing the sign Violet was holding.

"Oh, no," said Violet. "The cat belongs to someone else. We're just helping find her."

"You can put the sign up on the wall over there." Dr. Scott pointed. "I'll keep an eye out for her, too. Good luck."

"Thank you," said Henry. "By the way, Dr. Scott — has anyone else been in looking for a missing cat? A spotted one like Spotzie?"

Dr. Scott shook her head. "No one." A man came into the waiting room with a large, shaggy dog bouncing at the end of a leash. "Well, I need to get back to work. Good luck again."

The Aldens put the sign up on the wall and went back outside.

"Lunchtime?" said Benny hopefully.

"Not quite, Benny," said Jessie. She looked back over her shoulder, but the mysterious stranger had not reappeared. "We need to go see if Mr. Woods has a picture of Spotzie. That would help our search."

The Aldens rode their bicycles over to Mr. Woods's house. This time, when they got there, Mrs. Valentine opened the door when Henry knocked.

She smiled. "Hello," she said. "Come in." She led the way to the kitchen. A short young woman with lots of curly red hair was sitting at the kitchen table.

"This is my niece, Whitney," said Mrs. Valentine. "Whitney, these are the Aldens: Henry, Jessie, Violet, and Benny."

"How nice," said Whitney.

"It's nice to meet you, too," said Henry politely.

"I just made some cookies," said Mrs. Valentine.

"Cookies? I like cookies," said Benny.

Mrs. Valentine laughed. "I know you do, Benny. Mrs. McGregor has told me. Maybe you'd like some cookies now?"

"Yes, thank you," said Benny, promptly sitting down at the kitchen table.

Everyone laughed. While Henry helped pour milk into glasses, Jessie and Violet joined Benny and Whitney.

"We've been looking for Spotzie," Jessie told Whitney.

"Oh yes. Mr. Woods's cat. I've been hearing about her from my aunt. Any luck?" asked Whitney.

"Not yet," said Henry as he gave each of the Aldens a glass of cold milk. "We've made some signs and put them up at the animal shelter and at Dr. Scott's veterinary office and around town."

Mrs. Valentine put a plate of cookies warm

from the oven in the middle of the table, and she and Henry sat down, too. "It's very strange that the little cat disappeared like that off the front porch," Mrs. Valentine said.

"Maybe a dog came by and chased her off the porch while Mr. Woods was inside," suggested Whitney.

"A dog! We never thought of that," said Henry. "We thought she might have seen something and chased it and gotten herself lost somehow."

"An interesting theory," said Whitney, with a little smile. "You children are real detectives, aren't you?"

Benny didn't seem to notice Whitney's amused smile. "Yes," he said, reaching for another cookie. "We've solved a lot of mysteries. Do you want to help?"

"I'm kind of busy," said Whitney, raising her eyebrows. "I'm afraid you *children* will have to solve the mystery without my help."

Jessie's face turned red at Whitney's tone, but she didn't say anything. Instead, she turned to Mrs. Valentine. "We were wondering if Mr. Woods had a photograph of Spotzie. We want it to show to people."

"I'm sure he must," said Mrs. Valentine. "He's not home right now, but I'll asked him when he returns."

"Thanks," said Henry. "Well, it's time we were getting home."

The Aldens thanked Mrs. Valentine for the cookies and milk and said good-bye to Whitney.

"Nice meeting you, children," said Whitney. "Good luck with your little mystery."

The Alden children rode their bicycles slowly home.

"I don't think Whitney thinks we can solve the mystery," said Jessie. "She's nice, but she treated us like we were babies."

"Yes, but won't she be surprised when we do find Spotzie," answered Henry.

"Then she'll know we're real detectives," said Benny.

"Yes, Benny," said Jessie. "But even more important, Spotzie will be back home."

CHAPTER 5

Is This Spotzie?

The Aldens had just finished dinner. Jessie and Grandfather were playing checkers, while Henry read one of Benny's favorite stories to him. Violet had been listening, too, when the phone rang.

"I'll get it," she said. "Maybe it's another phone call about the signs we put up for Spotzie."

Grandfather Alden nodded. "Too bad those other phone calls weren't helpful."

Violet picked up the receiver. "Hello?"

"This the missing cat number?" growled a husky voice at the other end.

"Yes, it is," said Violet.

"Did you find her?"

"Not yet," Violet answered.

The husky voice went on, "Well, I'm missing a cat, too, see? And it looks like yours, see? So if you find my cat, like if someone calls you and says they've found a cat like mine, I'll give a reward. A *big* reward."

"What kind of cat?" asked Violet.

"You just let me know about *any* lost cats you hear about, okay? Write to, uh, Mr., uh, Jones, post office box ninety-three, Greenfield. Got that?"

"But . . ." Violet didn't get to finish. Mr. Jones had hung up the phone!

"Who was it, Violet?" asked Grandfather Alden.

Violet told the Aldens about the strange phone call. Everyone was puzzled.

"It sounded as if Mr. Jones wasn't his real name," said Violet. "Something about the way he said it sounded funny."

"But why would anyone call about a lost cat and use a phony name?" asked Jessie.

"It's another mystery!" exclaimed Benny.

"Or part of the same mystery, Benny," said Jessie.

Just then, the phone rang again. This time when Violet answered it, a brisk voice said, "I believe I've found your cat."

"You have?" said Violet. Quickly she explained that they didn't know exactly what Spotzie looked like. "We never met her. We're helping find her for someone."

"Oh," said the woman. "Well, I'm Professor Madison. You should come to my house tomorrow morning and get your cat."

Violet took Professor Madison's address and told her that the Aldens would be over to see her as soon as possible the next morning.

"Hillside Drive," said Henry. "That's a long way from where Spotzie and Mr. Woods live. How could a cat have gone so far?"

Violet clasped her hands. "Do you think it's Spotzie? I *hope* so."

"We'll find out tomorrow, first thing," Henry promised.

The next morning, the Aldens rode their bicycles to the other side of Greenfield, where Professor Madison lived. She had a low, rambling house set back from the road in an old pecan orchard. The house was painted blue, with lots of windows that had dark blue shutters. The front yard was neatly trimmed, but in the orchard, wildflowers grew beneath the trees and the grass was tall.

"I like this place," said Benny as the Aldens walked up the brick walk to Professor Madison's front door. "Look."

He pointed. In the window next to the door, a fat silver tabby cat sat, staring out at them.

Professor Madison opened the door immediately. "You must be the Aldens," she said quickly, before they could introduce themselves. She was a small, wiry woman wearing big silver hoop earrings and a big shirt over jeans. Her long dark hair was in a single braid down her back. "Come in."

She led the way down a wide hall to a sunny room at the back of the house. Behind them, the silver cat jumped down from the windowsill with a thump and followed.

When the Aldens reached the back room, they stopped and stared in amazement. Cats were everywhere. Cats were sleeping in the sun in the windows, cats were playing with toys on the floor, cats were sitting on bookshelves and chairs and on tops of cabinets. There seemed to be dozens of them.

"Wow," gasped Violet.

"My cat collection," said Professor Madison. She walked over to a big armchair and reached down and picked up a cat. "Here's your cat. I found her hiding in the bushes by my door a few days ago."

The Aldens looked at the cat in Professor Madison's arms. She was a little cat with a white stomach and feet. She had a blanket of orange and black spots on her back and her face was orange and black, too, with one orange ear and one black ear. She gazed up

at the Aldens with golden green eyes and began to purr.

"What a nice cat," said Violet. "Spotzie?" Violet reached out and petted the cat's head, and the cat purred even more loudly.

"Take her," said Professor Madison. "Here.Have a cardboard cat carrier you can have."

"But we're not sure she's the right cat," said Jessie.

"Has anyone else found a spotted cat and called you?" demanded Professor Madison.

"No," said Jessie.

"Then this is your cat." Before anyone could answer, Professor Madison marched out. She returned a few minutes later with a small cardboard cat carrier with handles on top and airholes in the side.

"Here," said the professor and thrust the carrier into Henry's arms.

"But what if it isn't Spotzie?" asked Benny.

The professor didn't answer. Instead, she led them back down the hall. "Thank you for coming," she said, and opened the front door.

The Aldens all looked at one another in surprise. At last Henry said, "Thank you."

"You're welcome," said Professor Madison, still holding the door open.

The Aldens walked out and the professor closed the door firmly behind them.

"That was strange," said Jessie.

"Maybe she was just very busy and didn't want to waste any time," Violet suggested.

"Spotzie?" asked Benny, bending down to look through one of the airholes in the cat carrier. The little cat inside meowed.

"Do you think it's her?" asked Violet. "Do you think she knows her name?"

"There's only one way to find out. We have to take her to Mr. Woods," said Henry.

Henry put the cat carrier in the large basket on his bike and carefully held it with one hand as he and the others rode back to Mr. Woods's house. As they walked up the front steps, Henry said softly, "Look! That curtain moved again."

They stopped in front of the door. Violet stepped back shyly. Henry raised his hand to knock. But he didn't get a chance. The door opened.

"Oh!" said Violet in surprise.

A man with shaggy brown hair, wearing wire-rimmed glasses, loose khaki pants, and a rumbled blue shirt stood there.

"Who are you?" he asked harshly.

The Aldens introduced themselves and explained that they had been looking for Spotzie. Mr. Woods listened without smiling.

Then Henry held up the cat carrier. "We think we might have found Spotzie," he said.

For one moment, Mr. Woods's whole face changed. He looked like a different person. A happy person. He grabbed the box from Henry and opened it.

His face changed back to its grumpy look. "No! That's not Spotzie! Spotzie is much, much prettier! How could you make such a stupid mistake?"

Suddenly Violet spoke. "We didn't know," she told Mr. Woods. "How could we know if we don't know what Spotzie looks like?"

"Much prettier!" Mr. Woods was almost shouting.

But Violet answered bravely, "If you could give us a picture of Spotzie, that would help."

Mr. Woods looked at Violet and frowned. "Wait here," he ordered rudely. Then he turned and walked back in the house.

He came back holding a small photograph. For a moment, he stood staring down at it. His grumpy expression changed to a sad one. "Smart," he said softly. "A smart little cat."

He looked up. "You know she could open any door, any latch? It was amazing to watch. And when I talked to her, she'd answer, just like she could understand what I was saying. She was special. Anyone could tell. Why, one day, when we were sitting on the porch, a complete stranger walked by and offered to buy her!"

Then Mr. Woods seemed to remember where he was. He shoved the photograph into Violet's hand. "Here," he said. "Not that I think it'll help. And you had better give that photograph back unharmed!"

Without even saying good-bye, Mr. Woods turned and walked back into his house and slammed the door.

CHAPTER 6

The Wrong Cat

"What do we do now?" asked Benny.

Henry looked at the closed door of Mr. Woods's house and then at Benny. He shook his head. "We'd better take this cat back to Professor Madison. But first, let's look at the photograph." The children looked closely at the picture of Spotzie.

"She has more black spots than this cat does," Jessie noticed.

"Yes, she does," Violet agreed.

The Aldens got back on their bicycles and began to make the long bike trip back to Professor Madison's house.

"Soo Lee is lucky she had a dentist appointment today," said Benny. "We're working *hard*."

"I'd rather be doing this than be at the dentist," said Violet.

They rode on. They were almost to Professor Madison's house when Violet pointed. "Look!"

A jogger was coming toward them. She was wearing shorts and a big T-shirt, and her curly red hair was pulled back in a ponytail.

"It's Whitney," said Henry in surprise. He waved.

Whitney saw the Aldens and waved back. She ran up to them and they pulled their bikes to the side of the road to wait for her.

"What are you doing all the way over here?" asked Jessie.

"My aunt lives in this neighborhood," said

Whitney. Just then, the little cat in the cat carrier meowed.

Whitney looked down. "Still working on your mystery?" she asked. "Or did you solve it?"

"Not yet," said Benny. "This is the wrong cat."

Whitney seemed amused. "What's been going on? I didn't know detectives made mistakes like that."

"Well," said Jessie, "we won't make it again. Now we have a picture of Spotzie that Mr. Woods gave us."

Violet pulled the picture out of her pocket and showed it to Whitney, while the others told Whitney about the odd phone call from Mr. Jones and the mysterious stranger who had followed them.

Whitney examined the photograph, then looked at the cat in the cat carrier. "That's a cute cat. She does look a lot like Spotzie."

"Mr. Woods doesn't think so. He said Spotzie is much prettier," Benny told Whitney. "And see? She has more black spots."

Whitney handed the photograph back to Violet. "Well, good luck with your mystery, children. I've got to keep jogging so I can stay in shape!"

"So you don't want to help us?" cried Benny.

Shaking her head, Whitney jogged quickly away.

"She doesn't believe us, does she," said Violet. "She doesn't believe we'll find Spotzie. But we will!"

More determined than ever, the Aldens continued on their way to Professor Madison's.

This time, they had to wait and wait before the professor finally opened her front door. She frowned when she saw them.

"What are *you* doing here?" she asked impatiently.

"We're bringing your cat back," Henry explained. "This isn't Spotzie."

The professor stepped back as if she might

close the door. But Henry put his hand on the door and stopped her.

"There must be some mistake," said Professor Madison.

"No, look. We have a picture of Spotzie now." Violet held the picture out, but Professor Madison didn't even glance at it.

"Even if it isn't your cat, you can keep her in place of Spotzie," said Professor Madison.

"But Mr. Woods doesn't want her. He wants his *own* cat. He wants Spotzie," Violet said.

"Do you have any other lost cats?" asked Benny.

"No! And I especially don't have a cat that looks like your cat. Go away! Now!" And with that, Professor Madison slammed the door!

For the second time that day, the four Alden children were left staring at a closed door.

"What's wrong with Professor Madison?"

LOST CAT

asked Benny. "Why doesn't she want this cat?"

"I don't know," said Jessie. "And how does she know she doesn't have a cat that looks like Spotzie when she wouldn't even look at the picture?"

"I don't know," said Henry. "I guess we'll have to take this cat home with us." Carrying the cat, he led the way back to the bicycles and the Aldens headed slowly home.

"It's a good thing it's not as hot today as it was the day that man followed us," said Violet as they rode their bicycles through town.

Jessie nodded. But she was thinking of something else. Suddenly she said, "Who was that man who followed us, anyway? Do you think it was Mr. Jones, the man who called about the lost cat?"

"It could be," said Henry. "But why? Why is he so interested in a lost cat? And what has that got to do with Spotzie?"

"Could he have had something to do with

Spotzie's disappearing?" asked Violet.

"Do you think he stole her?" asked Benny.

"I don't know." Jessie shook her head. "But even if he did, why is he looking for her now? And why was he following us?"

"And what about Professor Madison? Why is she acting so weird?" wondered Henry. "And how does she know what Spotzie looks like?"

The Aldens thought and thought, but they still hadn't come up with any answers by the time they'd reached home.

When the Aldens brought the little cat home, Watch was very interested. He tried to get close to her, but she arched her back and hissed at him. That made Watch bark. The cat jumped up on a bookcase, turned her back on Watch, and began to wash her paw.

"Oh, Watch," said Benny. "She doesn't want to be your friend."

But in spite of what Benny said, Watch stayed and watched the little cat for a long time. Violet put a bowl of food and water on top of the refrigerator where Watch couldn't reach it. Watch was very surprised when the cat jumped up there easily and began to eat her food. That made Watch bark again.

"Here, Watch," said Benny, and gave him a dog biscuit. Watch took it, gave the little cat one last curious look, and then trotted away.

"Tomorrow let's go over and talk to Dr. Scott again. Maybe she can help us," suggested Jessie.

"Good idea," said Henry.

Just then the phone rang. "Maybe someone has found Spotzie!" cried Violet.

But no one had. It was Soo Lee, calling to say she could help the Aldens look for Spotzie the next day. Violet told Soo Lee everything that had happened and of their plan to visit Dr. Scott again. Soo Lee said she would meet them there.

The cat finished her meal. She jumped down off the refrigerator. She walked to a chair and hopped up on it. After washing her ears, she curled up and went to sleep.

"Should we give her a name?" asked Violet.

Jessie shook her head. "I think we should wait. What if she belongs to someone else and already has a name?"

"But we can be thinking of names," said Henry.

"Oh, good," said Benny. Then he said, "Isn't it kind of strange — now we have a cat, but Mr. Woods still doesn't."

"Yes, Benny, it's still a mystery," said Violet with a sigh.

"Maybe we'll solve it tomorrow," said Benny.

"Maybe we will," said Henry, smiling at his little brother. "Maybe we will."

CHAPTER 7

So Many Cats!

Soo Lee was waiting by her bicycle at Dr. Scott's office when the Aldens got there the next morning. They had brought Watch with them to keep his mind off the strange cat who was living in his house.

Watch had followed happily on his leash, but when he saw where they were going, he stopped and sat down.

"Come on, Watch," said Henry.

Watch looked at Henry. Then he looked

at Dr. Scott's office building. At last he got up and walked over to Henry.

"Good dog, Watch," said Henry. He bent down and petted Watch's head. Soo Lee came over and petted Watch's head, too. Watch slowly wagged his tail.

The Aldens and Soo Lee went into Dr. Scott's office.

"May we see Dr. Scott?" asked Jessie.

"Is Watch sick?" asked Dr. Scott's assistant. She leaned over the counter to look down at Watch. Watch heard his name and looked up at her.

"No," said Henry. "We put that sign up the other day." He pointed to the sign about Spotzie on the bulletin board in Dr. Scott's office. "But no one has called. We thought Dr. Scott might have some ideas that would help us find Spotzie."

"Oh, yes. The missing cat." The assistant nodded. "Let me check and see if Dr. Scott can see you."

A moment later the assistant came back out. "Dr. Scott said to come on back to her office," she told the Aldens. She held the door open and the Aldens walked down the short hall past the examining rooms to Dr. Scott's office.

When the Aldens and Soo Lee came in, Dr. Scott set aside the papers she was looking at. "Hello," she said, smiling. "What can I do for you today?"

"Watch isn't sick," Benny explained quickly.

"My assistant told me it wasn't about Watch. She mentioned the missing cat. You still haven't found her?"

"Not yet," said Jessie. "We were hoping you might have some ideas."

Dr. Scott rubbed her chin. "Hmmm. You've checked the animal shelter?"

"Yes," said Henry. "We put a sign up there, too. But no one has brought in a lost cat like Spotzie."

"And you've looked all around where Spotzie was last seen?"

"Yes," Jessie answered Dr. Scott. "We

talked to everyone at every house on the street."

"Spotzie wasn't wearing a collar with an identification tag, was she?" asked Dr. Scott.

"No," said Henry.

Dr. Scott shook her head. "It's *very* important for pets to wear collars and identification tags."

"Even cats?" asked Benny.

"Even cats," said Dr. Scott. "There are even special stretchy collars for cats. If the cat climbs a tree and the collar gets caught, the cat can slip loose without being hurt."

"Wow," said Benny. "When we find Spotzie, we'll have to tell Mr. Woods."

"That's a good idea, Benny," said Dr. Scott. "Let me think . . . oh, yes. Do you know who Mr. Allen is?"

"No," said Henry. "Who is he?"

"A cat lover," said Dr. Scott. "He owns purebred cats and shows them in cat shows."

"Like dog shows?" asked Benny, remembering the dog show that had recently come to Greenfield and the mystery the Aldens had solved then.

"Sort of like dog shows," said Dr. Scott. "Mr. Allen is a specialist and a cat collector. He might be able to help. I'll give you his number."

Dr. Scott looked up Mr. Allen's phone number and wrote it down on a piece of paper.

"Thank you," said Jessie, carefully folding the paper and putting it into the pocket of her jeans.

"Good luck," said Dr. Scott. "Let me know what happens."

"We will," said Violet.

The Aldens and Soo Lee went back to the Aldens' house. Jessie called the number Dr. Scott had given them.

A man with a soft voice answered the phone.

Jessie explained who she was and why she had called. "Dr. Scott told us we should call you. She said you might be able to help," Jessie said.

Mr. Allen hesitated. Then after a long moment he said, "Well, I don't see how I can, but if you'd like to come over, you may." He told Jessie where he lived and hung up before Jessie could say thank you.

"I don't think he wanted to talk to us," said Jessie, hanging up the phone. She told her brothers and sister and Soo Lee about the conversation.

"Well, even if he didn't want to, he said he would," said Henry, when Jessie had finished. "We'd better get going before he changes his mind."

"You'll have to stay here, Watch," said Violet. "Mr. Allen has lots and lots of cats and you don't even like having one in your house."

Watch sat down as if he understood what Violet had said.

"Good dog, Watch," said Benny.

Saying good-bye to Watch and Mrs. McGregor, the children got their bicycles and pedalled over to Mr. Allen's house.

Like Mr. Woods's house, Mr. Allen's

house was at the end of a street. But it was very different. A high hedge surrounded the house so it could not be seen. Gates stood open on either side of the gravel driveway. The driveway was lined with neat flower beds.

As they rode their bicycles up the long driveway, the Aldens saw gardeners at work, one cutting the grass, another weeding the flower beds.

The enormous front door was made of dark polished wood. When Jessie knocked, a tall man with a stern expression answered.

"Mr. Allen?" asked Jessie.

"I am Mr. Allen's butler. Is Mr. Allen expecting you?" answered the butler.

"Yes," said Henry. "We called Mr. Allen about a missing cat."

The butler nodded his head slightly, then lifted his chin so that he seemed to be looking down his nose at the five children. "Walk this way, please," he said.

He led them down a long hall and into a room with a desk at one end. The room was lined with books. "I will inform Mr. Allen you are in the study."

"Wow," said Violet after the butler had left. "He's like a butler in the movies!"

"Do you think he likes his job?" asked Benny. "He didn't smile at all."

Henry shook his head. "Maybe butlers aren't supposed to smile, Benny."

"What a strange job!" exclaimed Benny.

Just then the door opened and a small round man wearing a dark blue suit with a red bow tie came in. He had a small mustache and thinning hair combed over a bald spot on the top of his head. He stopped near the door and peered at the Aldens over the top of his half-glasses.

"Yes?" he asked in a soft voice. "How do you think I can help you?"

"Mr. Allen?" asked Jessie again.

"I am he," said the man. "You must be the Aldens."

"Yes," Jessie said. Quickly she and the others introduced themselves.

"I don't see how I can help you with a

missing cat," said Mr. Allen. "All of my cats are here where they should be. I assure you, I would know if any cats were around that didn't belong."

Jessie stepped forward and held out the photograph of Spotzie. Mr. Allen bent and squinted down at it without taking the picture out of Jessie's hand.

"This is the lost cat, I presume," he said after a lengthy silence.

"It is!" burst out Benny. "Spotzie. She's lost and we have to find her so we can take her home."

"I wish I could be of help, young man. But my cats are registered purebreds, very valuable. Not a cat like this one."

"No spotted cats?" asked Benny.

"No." Mr. Allen shook his head, then hesitated. Finally he said, "Why don't you come see for yourself."

Once again, the Aldens found themselves following someone through the mansion. This time, Mr. Allen led them to a long, luxurious room.

Benny's eyes got very large when he saw the room. Like the back room at Professor Madison's house, it was filled with cats. But the room and the cats were very different.

The room seemed as big as Professor Madison's whole house. It was lined with cages. Most of the cages had the doors open so that the cats could come and go as they pleased. Every cage was elaborately decorated like a little house, with windows that had curtains. There was a nameplate on each door. Dishes with food and water sat in front of each cage. On the dishes were names that matched the nameplates on the cage doors. Toy mice and scratching posts and little balls and all kinds of cat toys were scattered everywhere.

A dainty silver cat with dark brown markings on her head, paws, and tail jumped down from atop a cat house and ran lightly toward them. She wound herself in and out between Mr. Allen's legs as he tried to walk.

Mr. Allen laughed and bent over to pet her. "There you go, Blue. This is Blue. She's a chocolate-point Siamese."

"Oh! Her eyes are blue," said Benny. "Is she still a kitten?"

"No, Siamese have blue eyes their whole lives," Mr. Allen told Benny.

"What kind of cat is that?" asked Soo Lee, pointing to a big white cat with long hair and a mashed-in face that made it look unhappy.

"That's Ralph. He's a champion long-haired Persian," said Mr. Allen, picking up the cat and stroking his luxurious fur. "In fact, all my cats are champions. However, some, like Blue, are retired. But as you can see, I have no cats like yours."

"You have so many different kinds!" exclaimed Jessie.

"My goal is to have at least one of every breed. And I very nearly do," said Mr. Allen, looking proud. "Cats are amazing creatures."

"I like cats, too," said Benny. "I like your cats. And Spotzie."

"I'm sorry I can't be of more help," said Mr. Allen. He led them back out of the cats' room and toward the front door. "Your cat is an ordinary cat, though, so it would be unlikely I would have her, don't you think? All my cats are rare and expensive."

"Every cat is special in its own way," said Violet loyally. "Including Spotzie."

Mr. Allen looked at Violet in surprise. A funny look came over his face. Then he said, "I'm sure she is," and led them all to the front door. He opened it. "If I hear anything at all about your cat, I'll certainly get in touch."

"Thank you," said Henry, and the five Aldens left.

No one said anything as they rode their bicycles home. There was nothing to say. Mr. Allen hadn't been able to help after all. They had seen lots of interesting cats, but they were no nearer to finding Spotzie than they'd been when they first started looking.

CHAPTER 8

A Strange Phone Call

"Look, Violet! That's the North Star," Henry pointed up at the sky.

The Aldens had just finished dinner and Grandfather Alden had gotten out his book of constellations. The four children were trying to find the constellations and stars he had shown them in the book.

"I see the Big Dipper," said Henry.

"Very good, Henry," said Grandfather.

Just then they heard the sound of the phone ringing through the open back door.

"I'll get it," said Henry.

He raced up the stairs and a moment later, the others heard the phone stop in mid-ring.

A few minutes later, Henry came back outside.

"Who was it, Henry?" asked Grandfather Alden.

"I don't know," said Henry. "I think someone was trying to disguise his — or her — voice."

"What do you mean?" Jessie asked quickly.

Henry said, "It was someone calling about Spotzie. The voice was very muffled and hard to hear. He — or she — said that Spotzie is lost and going to stay lost. And if we know what's good for us, we'll stop looking for her!"

Everyone was so surprised that no one said anything at all for a minute. Then Violet said, "Do you think it was the same man who called me? Mr. Jones?"

"There's no way of knowing," said Henry. "I couldn't tell if it was a man or a woman calling. But if it was a man, it might be the man you talked to."

Suddenly Jessie snapped her fingers excitedly. "But now we have a clue!"

"A clue?" Grandfather looked at Jessie. "What's the clue?"

"Now we know Spotzie was stolen! Why else would anyone want us to stop looking for her, unless they'd taken her and didn't want to get caught?" explained Jessie.

"You're right!" exclaimed Henry.

"Was it a cat burglar?" asked Benny, looking up at his grandfather. "Was it a cat burglar who took Spotzie?"

Grandfather Alden patted his youngest grandchild on the head. "It was a cat burglar of sorts, Benny."

"I think we should visit Professor Madison again," Jessie said. "I think she knows more than she is telling us."

The Aldens all agreed it was a good idea, and decided to go visit Professor Madison the following day.

* * *

The next day when the Aldens arrived at Professor Madison's, she was even more unfriendly than she had been before.

"Hello," said Henry politely when the professor opened the door.

This time, Professor Madison didn't try to close the door in their faces. Instead, she stepped outside onto her porch and shut the front door behind her. She folded her arms in front of her and frowned. "What is it now?" she asked.

"We'd like to talk to you about Spotzie." Jessie held up the photograph of Spotzie to remind the professor.

The professor sighed a big, annoyed sigh. "Are you still looking for that cat? Well, she's not here. Not now. Not ever!"

"Wait a minute," said Henry. "Remember the last time we were here and we tried to show you a photograph of Spotzie. You said you didn't have a cat that looked like ours. But you didn't really look at the photograph!"

Professor Madison bit her lip. "I saw as much as I needed to see."

"But — " Henry began.

"I've told you everything I'm going to tell you," Professor Madison told them.

"Then there *is* more," said Jessie quickly. "You know more and you aren't telling us!"

Putting her hand on the door handle behind her, the professor said,"No. Well . . ."

"Wait," said Violet. "Please wait. We need your help. We think Spotzie isn't lost after all. We think she was stolen. If you know anything that can help us find her, please tell us!"

The professor hesitated. She half turned, as if she were about to go back inside without answering. Then she turned back around.

"Okay," she said. "You're not the only one looking for a lost cat that matches the picture you showed me. The day before you came over, someone else was here looking for a lost cat. He'd gotten my name from the animal shelter as someone who had a lot of cats and might have taken his in."

"What happened?" asked Jessie eagerly.

"I showed him the cat I gave to you. He said she was his cat and made a grab for her. She hissed and tried to get away from him. That made me suspicious."

"Why would his own cat do that?" Benny's eyes were wide.

"I don't think it was his cat." Professor Madison went on, "I became really suspicious when he offered me a large reward for the cat — a great deal too much money — if I'd just hand her over. When I wouldn't, he became very angry and almost threatening. I made him leave.

"That same night, someone tried to break into my house. Fortunately, I have an alarm system and it scared off whoever it was. But I'm sure it was the same man."

"It could be the same man who called us, too," said Henry.

"What are you talking about?" the professor asked.

"Last night, someone called us and told us to stop looking for Spotzie if we knew what was good for us. That's what made us think she was stolen," Henry explained. "What did the man who came here look like?"

Professor Madison answered, "It was hard to tell. He was wearing a hat and dark glasses and a coat with the collar turned up — almost like a disguise. That made me suspicious, too."

The Aldens exchanged glances. It sounded like the man who had followed them outside the animal shelter!

"I think you're right," Professor Madison continued. "I think it might be the same man that called you." She reached out and took the photograph of Spotzie that Jessie was holding. "They do look alike, don't they. But I don't understand it. Why would someone steal a cat like this?"

No one could answer that.

The professor gave the photograph back to Jessie. "Anyway, I'm glad she's in a safe place now. That's why I insisted you take her. I know that man wasn't her owner and I didn't trust him."

Jessie put the picture carefully in her pocket. "Thank you, Professor Madison," she said.

"Good luck," said Professor Madison. "If anything else happens, or I can think of anything to help, I'll let you know."

She went back into her house and the Boxcar children went down the stairs and got back on their bicycles.

"Who could have taken Spotzie?" wondered Violet.

"And why?" added Jessie.

"That's the biggest mystery of all," said Henry. "Spotzie looks like an ordinary cat."

"Maybe she's not," said Benny. "Maybe she's a rare and valuable cat."

"Oh, Benny," said Jessie. "Spotzie isn't like those cats we saw at Mr. Allen's. Those cats are like the dogs we saw at the dog show. They are very valuable."

"But Watch isn't a show dog, and he's valuable," said Benny.

"That's true, Benny," Violet said. "And Spotzie isn't a show cat, but she is valuable to Mr. Woods, too, because he loves her, the same way we love Watch."

"That makes Watch and Spotzie the most valuable dog and cat of all," declared Benny.

"You're right," Violet said to her little brother, giving him a warm smile. "You're exactly right, Benny."

CHAPTER 9

Looking for Mr. Jones

As they turned down the street where they lived, Jessie suddenly exclaimed, "I have an idea! And I know it's going to help us solve this mystery!"

"What is it?" asked Violet.

"Yes, tell us," urged Henry.

"Remember that man who called you, Violet?" Jessie asked her sister.

"Mr. Jones." Violet nodded. "I remember."

"He gave you a post office box to write to.

Why don't we write him a letter and tell him we have a lost cat."

"But won't that be a lie?" said Violet.

"No!" crowed Benny. "Because we *do* have a lost cat. The cat Professor Madison gave us."

Jessie said, "That's right. And when Mr. Jones gets our letter, he'll call and we'll tell him to come over and we can see who he is and ask him a few questions."

"That's a terrific idea," said Henry.

"Thanks, Henry," said Jessie. "We'll write the letter this afternoon. If we take it to the post office, he might even get it tomorrow."

"We could have another clue by tomorrow!" cried Benny. "Hooray, hooray!"

"Don't say hooray yet," Jessie warned. "Let's see if this works."

That afternoon, right after lunch, the Aldens sat down at the kitchen table to write the letter. Henry did the writing, since he was the oldest, but everyone helped compose the letter. It read:

Dear Mr. Jones,

We have a lost cat like the one you were looking for. Please call us and you can come and see if she is yours.

Sincerely,

Henry, Jessie, Violet, and Benny Alden

Then Henry folded up the letter and carefully put their address on it. Grandfather Alden gave them a stamp and they walked down to the mailbox on the corner to mail it.

"We got here just in time," said Jessie, reading the sign on the mailbox. "The last time they pick up here is in fifteen minutes."

"Hurry, let's mail the letter!" Benny cried.

"Here, Jessie," said Henry. "You can mail it." He gave the letter to Jessie. Henry held the mailbox open and Jessie carefully pushed the letter in.

"Will Mr. Jones get the letter tomorrow?" asked Benny.

"I hope so," said Henry.

Benny looked at Henry seriously. "Spotzie has been away from home a long time. I'll bet she's homesick."

But no one called about Spotzie the next morning, although the Aldens all stayed home.

At lunch, Grandfather Alden looked around. "Why is everyone so quiet?" he asked.

"We still haven't found Spotzie," said Jessie.

"And we don't have any more clues," added Violet.

"You mustn't give up," said Grandfather.

"We won't," said Jessie. "But it's hard not to sometimes."

"Stick to it," said Grandfather. "That's the important thing."

Everyone nodded. They knew their grandfather was right. But it was hard not to worry.

Then, after everyone was finished with lunch, the phone rang.

"I'll get it!" cried Violet. She picked up the phone. "Hello?" She smiled. "Oh, hello Mr. Jones. You got our letter? Do you . . ." Violet's voice trailed off. The smile left her face. "Oh. Oh, I see. Are you sure? What kind of cat is yours? Mr. Jones? Hello? Mr. Jones?"

Slowly Violet hung up the phone.

"What is it?" demanded Jessie. "What did he say?"

Violet looked puzzled. "He said he'd found his cat. That we should keep the cat we have. She's probably a very nice cat. But when I tried to ask him about his cat, he hung up on me!"

"This is very strange," said Henry.

"What are we going to do *now*?" sighed Violet.

The Aldens went outside and sat down beneath the shade of an old oak tree by the old boxcar that had once been their home.

"What are we going to do now?" Violet repeated.

"Maybe we should talk to Professor Madison again," said Henry.

Jessie said, "It's true, she's acted pretty strangely. But if that man really was trying to break into her house and steal the cat, that would explain it."

"*If* she's telling the truth," said Henry.

"But why would Professor Madison steal a cat when she already has so many?" asked Violet.

"That's true," said Henry.

Suddenly Jessie said, "Whitney!"

Henry, Violet, and Benny looked at her in surprise. "What about Whitney?" asked Henry. "She couldn't have had anything to do with Spotzie's disappearance. Spotzie disappeared before Whitney ever arrived."

"But what if Whitney is the one making the mysterious phone calls? What if there is no Mr. Jones at all?" asked Jessie.

"Why would Whitney do that?" Benny wanted to know.

Jessie furrowed her brow. "Because . . . because she thinks we're just children and we can't solve this case. Maybe it's a practical joke?"

Benny shook his head. "It would be a mean joke!" he declared.

"I wonder if Whitney would do something like that?" said Violet. "I don't think she would."

After a moment, Jessie nodded her head in agreement with Violet. "You're right, Violet. I guess I don't think she would, either."

"Well, what about Mr. Allen?" suggested Henry. "Did you notice he seemed surprised when he saw Spotzie's photograph — almost as if he recognized her."

"That's true," Jessie said.

"Yes, he did act surprised," said Violet. "But why would he lie about ever having seen Spotzie?"

"Maybe *he* has Spotzie!" cried Benny.

"But why, Benny," said Jessie. "Why would he want Spotzie when he has so many other beautiful cats?"

"Mr. Jones, whoever he is, is the most likely 'cat burglar.' We have to find him to solve the mystery and find Spotzie."

"But how?" said Jessie. "How are we going to find Mr. Jones?"

Henry said, "Wait a minute. I've thought of a way we could find Mr. Jones."

"How?" cried Jessie excitedly.

"We wrote to him at a post office box," said Henry. "Box number ninety-three. All we have to do is watch the post office and see who comes to get the mail out of that box."

"Oh, Henry, that's a wonderful idea!" exclaimed Violet.

"We'll be like spies," said Benny. "Will we need disguises?"

Everyone smiled at that. "No, Benny," said Henry. "But we will be like spies, sort of, watching for Mr. Jones to see who he really is."

Benny nodded. "We can take Watch to *watch* for Mr. Jones."

"We'll do that," said Henry. "We can take turns, Benny. You and Watch and Jessie can watch tomorrow morning. Then Violet and I will come up to watch for a while."

"Can Soo Lee come, too?" asked Violet.

"Yes, of course," said Henry. "The more people we have helping us, the better!"

CHAPTER 10

The Chase Is On

Jessie, Benny, and Watch were waiting at the Greenfield Post Office when it opened the next morning. It was a bright, sunny day. The post office was surrounded by shady trees and had windows across the front.

Jessie, Benny, and Watch were about to go in and find box 93 when Jessie noticed a sign on the post office door: NO DOGS ALLOWED.

"You and Watch will have to wait out

here," she said, pointing to the sign. Benny sounded out the words slowly and then looked at his sister.

"Why aren't dogs allowed in the post office?" he asked. "I don't like that rule!"

"I don't either, Benny, but we have to obey it."

"Okay," said Benny, taking Watch's leash. "We'll wait out here. Maybe we'll even catch Mr. Jones while you're inside."

Jessie went inside the post office and quickly found box 93. It was midway up a row of boxes and it could be seen through the front window of the post office.

She hurried back out and showed Benny which box it was. "We can sit here under this tree and keep our eyes on the mailbox," she said.

"Oh, good," said Benny, sitting down.

Jessie sat down next to Watch and Benny, and leaned back against the tree. For a little while, the post office was very busy as people stopped by on their way to work. Then fewer people came. Several customers went to check their mail, but no one went to box number 93.

Benny yawned. "I'm tired," he said. "We've been here a long, long time."

"Henry and Violet and Soo Lee will come soon," said Jessie. She watched a stout woman in a baseball cap walk up to the wall of mailboxes. Her heart beat faster in excitement. Was Mr. Jones really *Ms.* Jones?

But the woman reached up high and opened a mailbox in the corner. Jessie leaned back against the tree again.

Watch, who had been taking a nap next to Benny, lifted his head and barked.

"What is it, boy?" asked Benny. "Is it Mr. Jones?"

"I think it's just a squirrel Watch wants to chase," said Jessie, pointing.

Sure enough, a squirrel who had been hopping over the ground scurried up a nearby tree. Watch laid his head back down on his front paws.

The time seemed to pass very, very slowly. Jessie was glad when she stood up to stretch and saw Henry and Violet and Soo Lee riding their bicycles down the sidewalk toward them.

"Any luck?" asked Henry as they came to a stop near the tree.

Jessie shook her head. She showed them where box 93 was located. "No one has come near it," she said. "I'm glad you're here. We were getting tired."

"And hungry," said Benny.

"Well you can take a break now," said Henry.

Violet set her backpack down on the ground and reached inside. "Here, Benny, I have an apple for you," she said.

"Thanks!" said Benny.

Just then Soo Lee grabbed Jessie's arm. "Look!" she said.

They all looked in the direction Soo Lee was pointing. Someone wearing an overcoat, dark glasses, and gloves, with a hat pulled low over his eyes was walking toward the wall of mailboxes.

Violet gasped. "That looks like the person

who followed us that day!"

"And like the person Professor Madison described," said Henry.

As they watched, the person reached out and opened box number 93!

"It's him," said Henry.

Mr. Jones took out a single letter and ripped it open hastily, throwing the envelope to the floor.

"He's littering," said Benny indignantly.

"Wait a minute, Benny. Let's see what happens," Jessie told her younger brother.

Mr. Jones read the letter. Then he folded it up and stuck it in his pocket, and began to walk very fast toward the post office door.

"We can follow him," Jessie said. "Everybody get your bicycles ready."

But it was no use. When Mr. Jones got outside the post office, he went to a big, dark car parked in front of the post office. Before the Aldens could do anything, he had jumped inside and sped away.

The children jumped on their bicycles and rode as fast as they could after the car. But

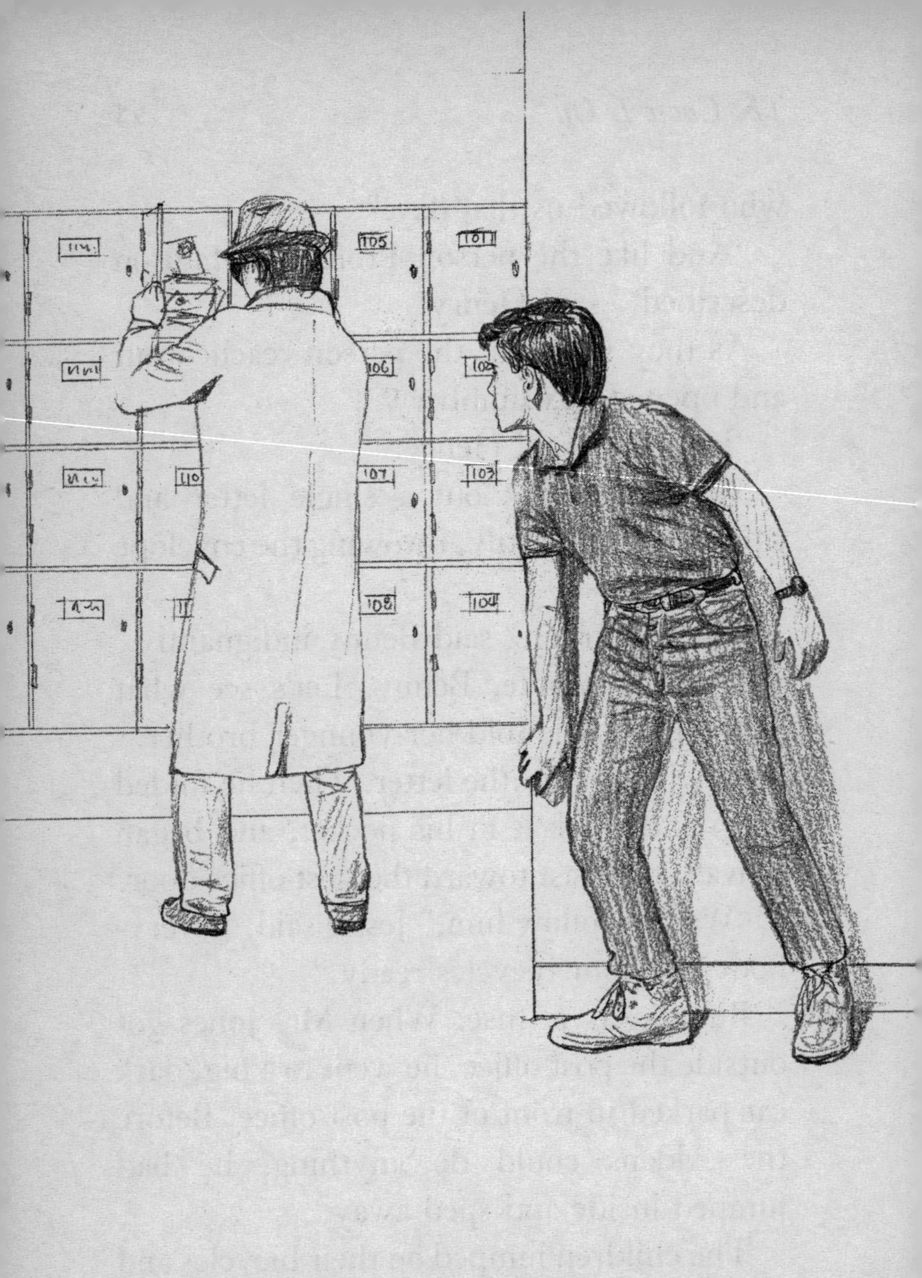
105
101
106
107
103
108
104

by the time they'd gone a block, the car had disappeared from sight.

"Oh, no!" said Henry. "We've lost him!"

"We'll never solve this mystery!" cried Violet.

"Yes, we will," panted Jessie, pulling her bicycle to a stop. "Remember what Grandfather said about not giving up."

"What can we do?" asked Soo Lee.

"We'll just have to watch the post office again tomorrow," answered Jessie. "And the next day. And the next. For as many days as it takes."

Benny made a face. Then he said, "But what about the envelope?"

"The envelope?" asked Violet.

"The envelope Mr. Jones threw on the floor. Maybe it has a return address on it," said Benny. "Maybe that's where Mr. Jones was going!"

"Benny, you're a genius!" cried Jessie happily.

Benny blushed and grinned. "Thank you," he said.

Jumping back on their bicycles, the Aldens raced back to the post office. Sure enough, the envelope that Mr. Jones had wadded up and thrown on the floor was still there.

Benny bent over and picked it up and smoothed it out.

They all crowded around and read the return address on the wrinkled envelope that Benny was holding.

"It's from Mr. Allen!" said Jessie in amazement.

"And Mr. Jones drove off in that direction," added Henry.

"I bet I know what we do now," said Benny. "We go to Mr. Allen's!"

"You're right," said Jessie. "Mr. Allen, here we come!"

Without wasting another moment, the children got on their bicycles and pedalled as fast as they could to Mr. Allen's house. In a short time, they were turning up the long gravel driveway.

"There's Mr. Jones's car," said Violet. Sure enough, the same big, dark car that they'd watched Mr. Jones leave the post office in was parked by the front door of the house.

The Aldens left their bicycles out of sight by the side of the house, and Benny tied Watch to a nearby tree.

"Wait here," he said, holding a finger to his lips. "And don't bark. We're about to solve a mystery!"

CHAPTER 11

A Rare Cat Indeed

The butler answered the door just as he had before.

"May I help you?" he asked as if he had never met them.

"We're here to see Mr. Allen," said Jessie politely.

"Is he expecting you?" asked the butler haughtily.

"No, but it's very important," Jessie told the butler.

The butler looked down his long nose at

the five children. At last he nodded his head slightly. "Very well. If you will step this way."

This time, he didn't take them to the library. He took them to a small room just off the front part of the hall.

"If you will wait here, I will see if Mr. Allen can see you. It may be a few minutes. He is in a meeting and does not wish to be disturbed."

"Thank you, we can wait," said Jessie.

The butler gave a disapproving sniff and closed the door firmly behind him.

"Do you think Mr. Allen is meeting with Mr. Jones?"asked Violet as soon as the butler had closed the door.

"I'm sure he is," said Jessie.

"I bet I know where, too," said Henry. "Remember that room that the butler took us to the last time we were here? The one with the desk and the books in it?"

"Yes!" Jessie gave Henry a thumbs-up sign. "I bet you're right, Henry. Come on, everybody."

"Are we going to be spies now?" asked Benny.

"Yes, we are," said Violet, taking Benny's hand. Quickly and quietly, the five children crept out of the room and down the long hall to the library door. Jessie looked both ways. Then, very slowly, she turned the handle of the door. She did it so carefully that no one would have noticed it turning from the other side. At last she was able to push the door open a crack. The sound of voices came through the crack. The children all leaned forward and began to listen.

"Gimme the money like you promised," growled a voice. "I got you your cat."

"Very well," said the soft voice of Mr. Allen. "Although why I should pay you anything is beyond me. You almost botched the whole job, losing the cat like that."

"I didn't lose her," growled the voice. "She got away. I dunno how she did it, but she got the door of her cat carrier open!"

The Aldens all looked at one another, remembering what Mr. Woods had said about

Spotzie being able to open any latch or door. They had to be talking about Spotzie!

Mr. Allen snorted. "Very well, I'll pay you, Kramer. I'm a man of my word. Here . . ."

"Someone's coming," whispered Henry.

"Come on!" said Jessie. She pushed the door open and the five children rushed into the room.

The two men standing by the desk froze. One was Mr. Allen, wearing a suit and a blue bow tie. The other was the man they'd been calling Mr. Jones. He was still wearing his coat and dark glasses, but he'd taken his gloves and hat off. Between them on the floor sat a cat carrier with a small padlock on the door.

"You, you . . ." sputtered Mr. Allen. "What are you doing here?"

"Looking for a lost cat," said Jessie. She pointed to the cat carrier. "*That* cat!"

"My butler will handle this," said Mr. Allen, regaining his calm. "I'll ring for him."

"Then you'd better ring for the police, too, because that's a stolen cat!" said Jessie.

Mr. Allen stared at the five children. They stared back. What would Mr. Allen do?

Slowly, Mr. Allen walked over to a chair and sat down. He put his head in his hands. "It's true," he said.

Benny bent down and looked in the cat carrier. From inside, they all heard an indignant *meow*. "She looks just like Spotzie's picture," said Benny.

Hearing her name, Spotzie meowed again.

"It is, er, Spotzie. Yes, I'm afraid it is," said Mr. Allen. "You see, I saw her on one of my walks and I had to add her to my collection."

"But why?" asked Violet.

Mr. Allen raised his head. "I told you she was just an ordinary cat. But that's not true. I think she's rare. A very rare cat indeed."

Violet said, "She's the only Spotzie in the world. She's Mr. Woods's only friend. He loves her very much and he misses her. How could you do that to someone? How could you steal their cat?"

"You don't understand," Mr. Allen told Violet. "This cat is a curly-coated cat. That in itself is fairly rare. There are only two kinds of curly-coated cats, of the type known as *rex*, in the cat show world. But I think Spotzie might be a third type, which would make her very rare and valuable indeed."

"Wow," said Benny. "I didn't know cats could have naturally curly hair."

Mr. Allen went on. "I saw her and I wanted her for my collection. I offered her owner money, but he wouldn't part with her for any amount of money. Then I happened to mention her to Mr. Kramer here. I'm afraid Mr. Kramer got carried away and, er, stole the cat from Mr. Woods's porch."

"That's not true," snarled Mr. Kramer. "You paid me for this job, you know you did. Besides, you can't prove anything anyhow! I found the cat, see? And I wanted to bring her to you 'cause she looked weird and I knew you liked weird cats."

Mr. Allen waved his hand. "I won't argue with you here, Kramer. It's beside the point."

"It *was* you," said Henry to Mr. Kramer. "You followed us that day we left the animal shelter."

Mr. Kramer nodded. "Yeah. After I, uh, found the cat, she got away from me. Then I saw your signs. So I thought I'd follow you to see if you knew anything I didn't. But you spotted me."

"You went to Professor Madison's, too, looking for Spotzie," said Henry.

"Yeah. I was sure she was holding out on me, that she had that crazy cat, but I guess she didn't," said Mr. Kramer.

"And you called us to offer a reward to find her," said Violet.

Mr. Kramer nodded again. "She was still missing. But then I found her wandering around town. I didn't need you looking for her. That's when I gave you the warning." He looked puzzled. "But how did you find me, anyway?"

"We followed you from the post office," said Benny. "You threw the envelope on the floor. It had Mr. Allen's name on it." Benny folded his arms and stared at Mr. Kramer sternly. "You shouldn't litter!"

Mr. Allen interrupted. "If you children are sure this is the cat you're looking for, of course I'm willing to return her to you. I certainly don't want any trouble over this."

"You're a bad man," said Benny. "You're a bad man to steal something. Especially Mr. Woods's cat!"

The children looked at one another. They had no real proof of what Mr. Kramer and Mr. Allen had done. And they had found Spotzie.

"Okay," said Henry. "Give us the key to the lock on her cat carrier and we'll be going."

Mr. Kramer reached in his pocket and pulled out a key. "All that work for nothing!" he said. "And her getting out and me having to chase her all over town. All for nothing."

"Oh, be quiet!" snapped Mr. Allen.

Violet took the key and put it in her

pocket. Henry picked up the cat carrier and the five children turned to go. At the door they stopped and turned to look back.

"If anything — anything at all — like this ever happens again," warned Jessie, "we'll know it's you and we'll go to the police."

Neither man answered.

"Come on," said Henry. "Let's take Spotzie home."

CHAPTER 12

Found at Last

"We found her, we found her!" shouted Benny happily as the children walked into the house. Watch barked along with Benny.

Grandfather looked up from the newspaper he was reading. "What is it, Benny?"

"We found Spotzie!"

Grandfather put down his paper. "That's wonderful."

"Here she is," said Henry, setting down the cat carrier. "But we'd better keep her in there until Mr. Woods gets her. We wouldn't want to lose her again."

"I'm going to call Mr. Woods right now," said Violet. "And Professor Madison, too!"

Grandfather bent over to look in the cat carrier. "She's a pretty cat, but her coat looks funny."

"She's a very rare cat, Grandfather," said Jessie. "A curly-coated cat."

"Is that so? How do you know that?" asked their grandfather.

Quickly, Jessie and Henry and Benny and Soo Lee told Grandfather Alden everything that had happened. Just as they were finishing, Violet came back in. "Mr. Woods hardly let me say 'We found Spotzie' before he said he'd be right over! And Professor Madison said she'd come over and get her cat, too," she reported.

A few minutes later the doorbell rang. When Henry opened it, Mr. Woods rushed into the room. "Where is she!" he cried. "Where's Spotzie?"

"Right here," said Violet. She got the key

and bent down and unlocked the door of the cat carrier. A small calico cat with shiny wavy fur poked her head out.

"Spotzie!" cried Mr. Woods. "It *is* you."

The cat heard Mr. Woods's voice. "Meow!" she cried. She bounded across the living room to him, her tail held high like a flag. A moment later, Mr. Woods was holding Spotzie in his arms. "Good girl, good Spotzie," he crooned. Spotzie purred loudly, her eyes half closed with pleasure.

Mr. Woods looked up at last. "You did find her! I didn't believe you could, but you did!"

"She wasn't lost," said Jessie, "she was stolen. But you should still get her a collar and identification tags."

"Yes," said Benny. "Dr. Scott said they even make special stretch collars for cats so they can't get them caught in trees or anything."

Mr. Woods listened to what Benny and Jessie were saying, then answered, "I'll do that. First thing tomorrow morning Spotzie

will get a new collar and I'll order her some identification tags. Would you like that, Spotzie?"

Spotzie purred even more loudly and Mr. Woods grinned. When he smiled, he seemed like a different person. "But what is this about her being stolen?"

The Aldens were just about to explain what had happened, when the doorbell rang again. A moment later, Professor Madison walked in with a cat carrier in one hand. Henry introduced Professor Madison to Mr. Woods and Grandfather Alden.

"Spotzie was stolen," said Mr. Woods to Professor Madison.

"Ah, yes. You had thought she might be," said Professor Madison to the Aldens and Soo Lee. "What happened?"

"Well, you see," began Jessie. But she didn't get to finish her sentence before the doorbell rang again!

"Who can it be now?" wondered Violet. She didn't have long to wait for an answer. Whitney came bounding into the living room, dressed in her jogging clothes.

"I stopped by to visit my aunt and she told me you guys had found the lost cat. Good work," said Whitney. "So, what's the story?"

The five children looked at one another and began to laugh. Then Jessie said, "Well, you see . . ."

This time, no doorbell interrupted Jessie. She got to finish her story, with the help of Henry, Violet, Benny, and Soo Lee, and an occasional bark from Watch.

"So you're a very valuable cat, eh?" Mr. Woods said to Spotzie. "I knew that already!"

"What are you going to do with her?" asked Whitney. "Are you going to sell her for a lot of money?"

Mr. Woods shook his head. "Oh, no," he said. "But I am going to take her into Dr. Scott tomorrow and see if it is true about her being a rare cat, and to make sure she is in good health after being gone so long. But whether Spotzie is a rare cat or not, she's worth more than any money in the world to me!" He looked over at the five Aldens. "Thank you so much for finding her."

"I didn't think you kids could do it," said Whitney, "but I see I was wrong."

"You did an excellent job," said Professor Madison. "Well, I guess I better take that other little cat home. Unless you want to keep her?"

Just then, the little cat came strolling into the living room.

"Woof!" said Watch, and leaped toward her.

"Whoa, Watch!" cried Benny, catching Watch's collar.

The little cat flattened her ears, then looked all around.

"Meow!" said Spotzie and jumped out of Mr. Woods's arms. She trotted lightly over to the little cat and they touched noses. A moment later they were racing around the room playing.

"I wish we could keep her," said Grandfather Alden. "But Watch doesn't seem to want a cat in his house."

"Too bad," said Professor Madison. "I can see you would give her a good home, and I have too many cats as it is."

Mr. Woods thoughtfully watched the two cats racing around and around the room. Then he said, "Well . . . maybe Spotzie would like someone to play with. And for that matter, what could it hurt to have another little cat in the house?"

Professor Madison said, "That's how I started: one cat, then another . . ."

Then Mr. Woods did an unexpected thing. He laughed aloud!

The five children looked at one another in amazement. This wasn't the same grumpy Mr. Woods they'd first met!

"Maybe that will happen to me," said Mr. Woods. He squatted down. "Here, kitty. What do you call her, Professor Madison?"

"I hadn't named her yet. I was hoping I'd find a home for her," said the professor, kneeling down next to Mr. Woods.

"Maybe we could think of one together,"

said Mr. Woods. "Would you help me carry her home?"

"I'd be glad to," said Professor Madison.

"Great," said Whitney, watching the whole scene. "Listen, I've got to keep running, but hey, if I ever have a mystery that needs solving, I'll think of you guys." With a wave of her hand, she jogged out of the room. A moment later they heard the front door close.

Henry, Violet, Jessie, and Soo Lee helped Mr. Woods and Professor Madison put the cats into their cat carriers while Benny held Watch.

"How can I ever thank you?" asked Mr. Woods.

"Maybe we could come visit Spotzie and her friend some time?" asked Violet shyly.

Mr. Woods smiled cautiously at Violet. "I'd like that," he told her. "You are all welcome to come visit anytime."

Watch barked and Mr. Woods looked over at him. "You, too, Watch. But you'd better not chase any cats!"

"I won't let him," promised Benny, still holding on to Watch's collar.

Mr. Woods and Professor Madison walked out the front door holding their cat carriers.

"Oh, good." Violet sighed a happy sigh. "We found Spotzie."

"And a home for the little cat," said Soo Lee.

"And Mr. Woods found a new friend and so did Spotzie," said Jessie.

"And we solved the mystery," said Benny.

"We sure did, Benny," said Henry. "We sure did!"

Gertrude Chandler Warner discovered when she was teaching that many readers who like an exciting story could find no books that were both easy and fun to read. She decided to try to meet this need, and her first book, *The Boxcar Children*, quickly proved she had succeeded.

Miss Warner drew on her own experiences to write the mystery. As a child she spent hours watching trains go by on the tracks opposite her family home. She often dreamed about what it would be like to set up housekeeping in a caboose or freight car — the situation the Alden children find themselves in.

When Miss Warner received requests for more adventures involving Henry, Jessie, Violet, and Benny Alden, she began additional stories. In each, she chose a special setting and introduced unusual or eccentric characters who liked the unpredictable.

While the mystery element is central to each of Miss Warner's books, she never thought of them as strictly juvenile mysteries. She liked to stress the Aldens' independence and resourcefulness and their solid New England devotion to using up and making do. The Aldens go about most of their adventures with as little adult supervision as possible — something else that delights young readers.

Miss Warner lived in Putnam, Connecticut, until her death in 1979. During her lifetime, she received hundreds of letters from girls and boys telling her how much they liked her books.